INSTANT WALL ART:

BOTANICAL PRINTS

45 READY-TO-FRAME VINTAGE
ILLUSTRATIONS FOR YOUR HOME DÉCOR

Adams Media
New York London Toronto Sydney New Delhi

Adams Media
An Imprint of Simon & Schuster, Inc.
57 Littlefield Street
Avon, Massachusetts 02322

ADAMS MEDIA and colophon are trademarks of Simon and Schuster.

For information about special discounts for bulk purchases, please contact Simon & Schuster Special Sales at 1-866-506-1949 or business@simonandschuster.com.

The Simon & Schuster Speakers Bureau can bring authors to your live event. For more information or to book an event contact the Simon & Schuster Speakers Bureau at 1-866-248-3049 or visit our website at www.simonspeakers.com.

Interior illustrations © alephcomo/123RF; iStockphoto.com/nicoolay; and Lunagirl Images.

Manufactured in the United States of America

10

Library of Congress Cataloging-in-Publication Data has been applied for.

ISBN 978-1-4405-8566-1

Contains material adapted and abridged from *The Art of Nature Coloring Book* by Adams Media, copyright © 2013 by Simon & Schuster, Inc., ISBN 978-1-4405-7060-5.

Introduction

Today, beautifully colored nature prints are showing up everywhere you look—from popular design magazines and websites to the walls of your friends' living rooms and kitchens. And now, instead of having to choose between one or two expensive prints, you can choose from the forty-five beautiful illustrations found within the pages of *Instant Wall Art: Botanical Prints* to personalize your own walls!

Extraordinarily popular in the eighteenth and nineteenth centuries, these types of prints were first drawn and hand-colored by botanists, who used the lovely pastel shades of watercolors to capture the scientific details of the flora they studied. Now, with images ranging from the blooming Cape blue water lily to the juicy pear to the vibrant cacao tree, you're sure to find something in this book that speaks to your design aesthetic. These nature prints measure 8" × 10" and will fit in a standard mat and frame once removed from the book at the perforated edge. So choose the prints you love, hang them on your walls, and enjoy the elegance of nature in your own home, year-round!

THE
PRINTS

Geum reptans L.

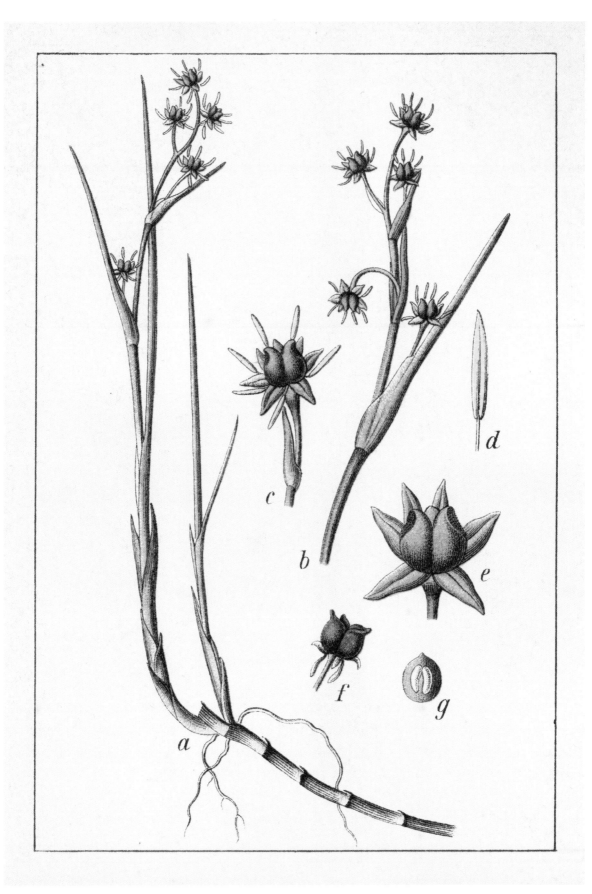

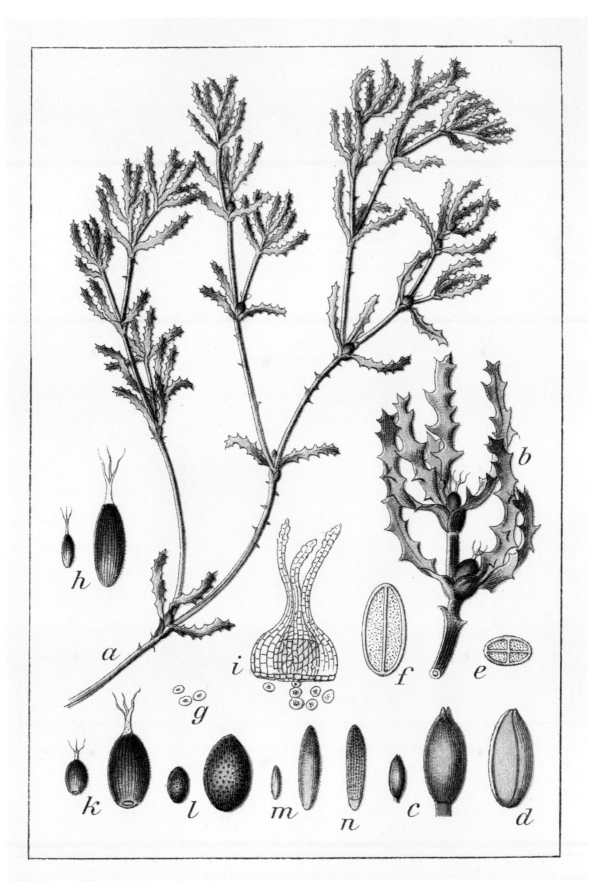

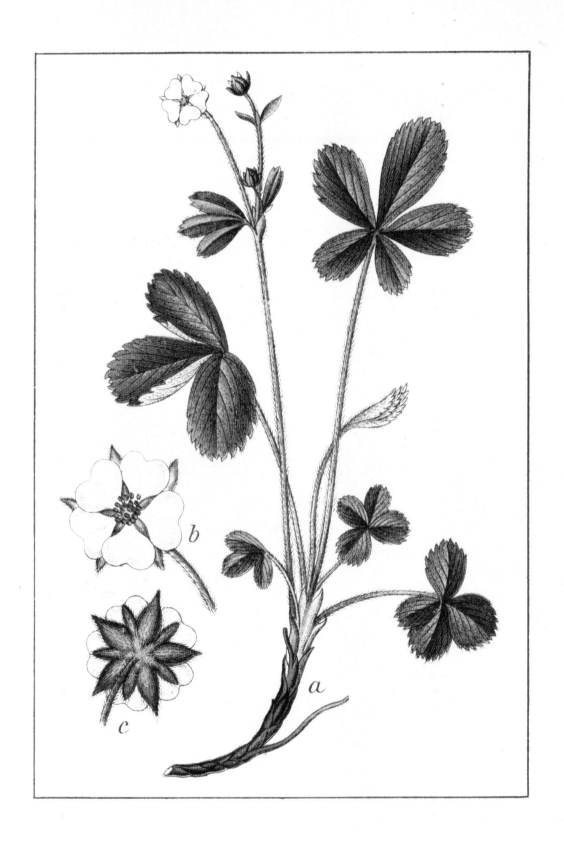

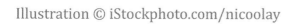

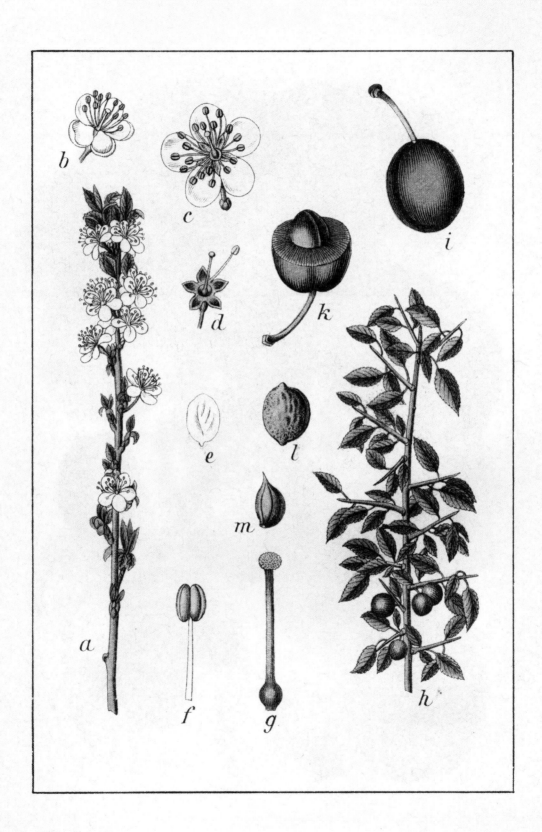

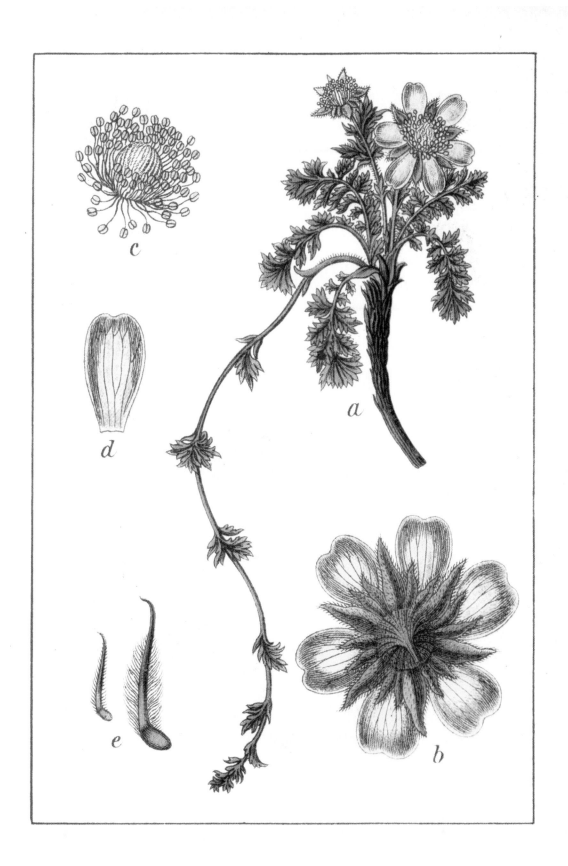

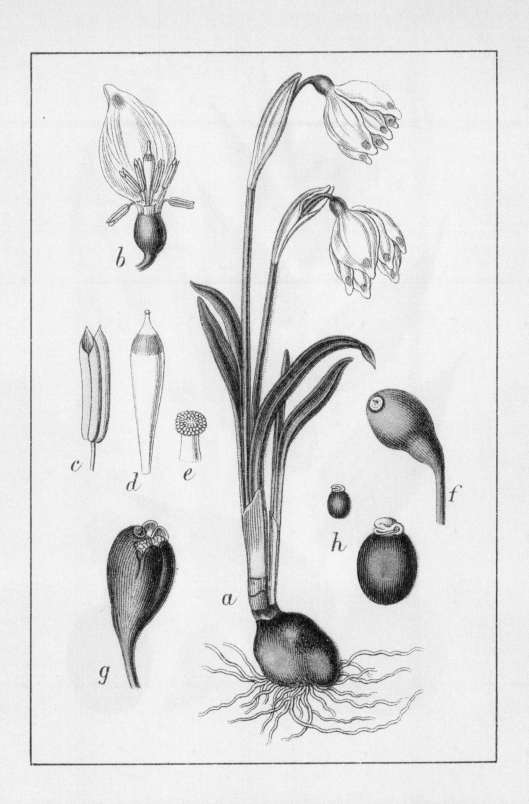

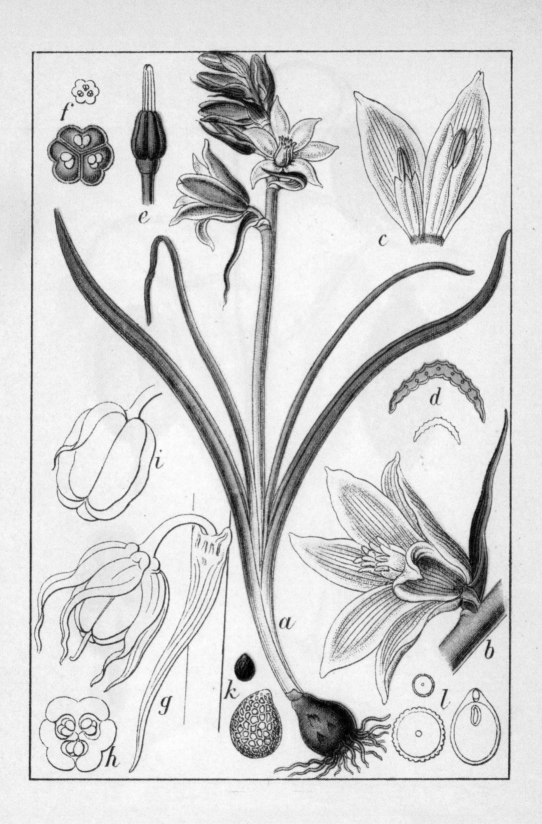

LAGERSTRŒMIA REGIA Roxb.

MANGIFERA INDICA L.

CITRUS DECUMANA.

THEOBROMA CACAO

BUTEA FRONDOSA. Roxb.

Anémone simple.   Anemone simplex.

GARCINIA MANGOSTANA L. Mangues

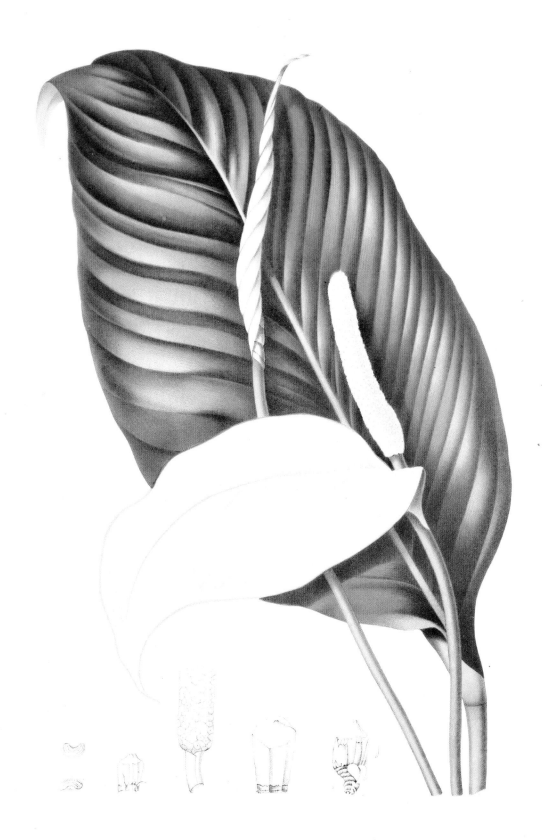

SPATHIPHYLLOPSIS MINAHASSAE T.&B. Tjariang Poetie

MUSA PARADISIACA L.

OTOPHORA ALATA BL.

AMHERSTIA NOBILIS WALL.

POINCIANA REGIA BOJ.

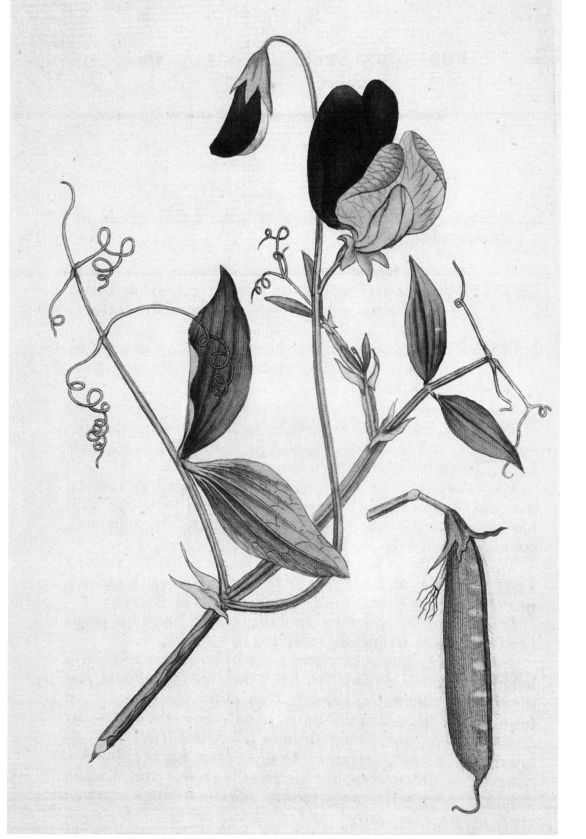

Pub. as the Act directs. Mar. 1.1790, by W.Curtis. Botanic-Garden, Lambeth-Marsh.

Syd: Edwards del. Pub. by T. Curtis, Stone Crescent Dec 1. 1805. F.Sansom sculp

Syd: Edwards del. Pub. by T. Curtis, St Geo: Crescent Oct. 1. 1803. F.Sansom sculp